Exploring Citizenship

Making Choices

Vic Parker

Heinemann Library,
Chicago, IL

www.heinemannraintree.com

Visit our website to find out more information about Heinemann-Raintree books.

To order:

☎ Phone 888-454-2279

💻 Visit www.heinemannraintree.com to browse our catalog and order online.

Edited by Rebecca Rissman and Catherine Veitch
Designed by Ryan Frieson and Betsy Wernert
Picture research by Elizabeth Alexander and Rebecca Sodergren
Production by Duncan Gilbert
Originated by Heinemann Library
Printed in China by South China Printing Company Ltd

Library of Congress Cataloging-in-Publication Data
Parker, Victoria.
  Making choices / Vic Parker.
      p. cm. -- (Exploring citizenship)
  Includes bibliographical references and index.
  ISBN 978-1-4329-3317-3 (hc) -- ISBN 978-1-4329-3325-8 (pb)
  1. Choice (Psychology)--Juvenile literature. 2. Decision making--Juvenile literature. I. Title.
  BF611.P36 2009
  170'.44--dc22
                              2008055310

Acknowledgments

We would like to thank the following for permission to reproduce photographs: Alamy **pp. 4** (© Jupiterimages/Bananastock), **10** (© David Hoffman Photo Library), **11** (© Janine Wiedel Photolibrary/Judy Chapman), **16** (© Varina Patel), **19** (© bildagentur-online/begsteiger), **20** (© Sally & Richard Greenhill), **22** (© Radius Images), **23** (© Roel Meijer), **24** (© Jupiterimages/ Bananastock), **26** (© Radius Images); Corbis **pp. 21** (© Matthias Tunger/zefa), **13** (© Gideon Mendel), **27** (© Bryan Allen); Getty Images **pp. 5** (Jamie Grill/Iconica), **6** (Piotr Sikora/Photonica), **8** (Andersen Ross/Blend Images), **15** (Jack Hollingsworth/ Photodisc), **12** (Ricky John Molloy/Stone), **29** (Lori Adamski Peek/ Stone); Science Photo Library **pp. 18** (Michael Donne), **14** (Ian Hooton); Shutterstock **pp. 7** (© Wouter Tolenaars), **9** (© Mandy Godbehear).

Cover photograph of a girl looking at a salad and a chocolate cake reproduced with permission of Corbis (© Fancy/Veer).

The publishers would like to thank Yael Biederman for her help in the preparation of this book.

Every effort has been made to contact copyright holders of any material reproduced in this book. Any omissions will be rectified in subsequent printings if notice is given to the publisher.

All the Internet addresses (URLs) given in this book were valid at the time of going to press. However, due to the dynamic nature of the Internet, some addresses may have changed, or sites may have changed or ceased to exist since publication. While the author and publisher regret any inconvenience this may cause readers, no responsibility for any such changes can be accepted by either the author or the publisher.

Contents

Some words are shown in bold, **like this**. You can find out what they mean by looking in the glossary.

What Is Citizenship?

Citizenship is about being a member of a group such as a family, a school, or a country. A citizen has **rights** and **responsibilities**. Having rights means there are certain ways that people should treat one another.

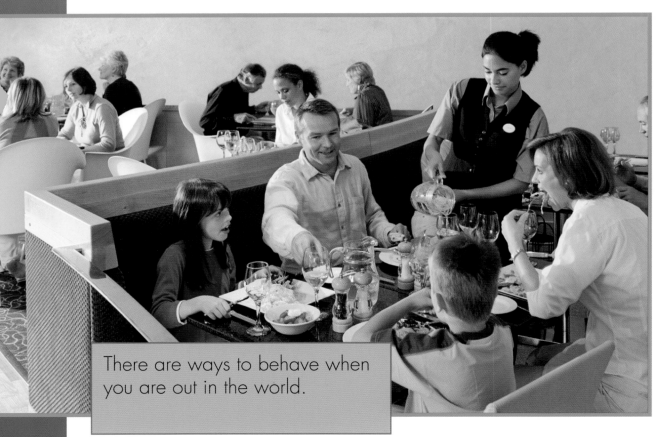

There are ways to behave when you are out in the world.

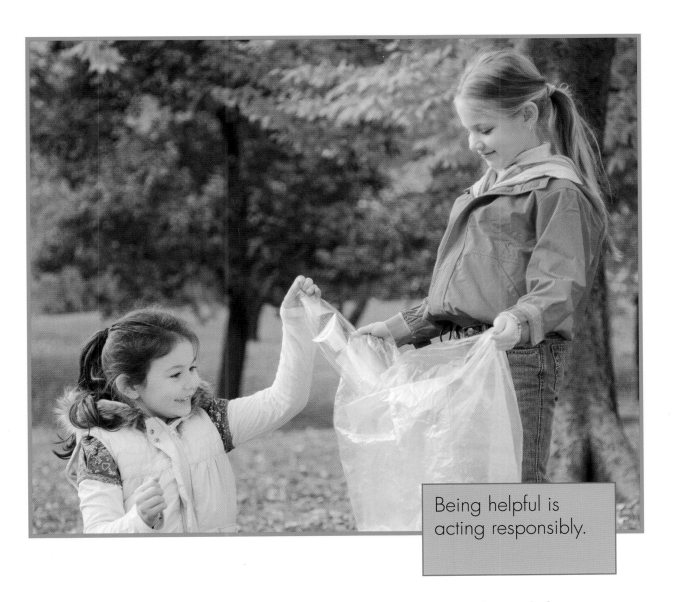

Being helpful is acting responsibly.

Having responsibilities means you should act or behave in a certain way. The way you behave affects other people. At home and in school you have rights and responsibilities.

What Are Choices?

Choices are decisions we make about what we want to do. Every day, we all have to make many choices in our lives. Some choices are not very important, such as what color socks we are going to put on.

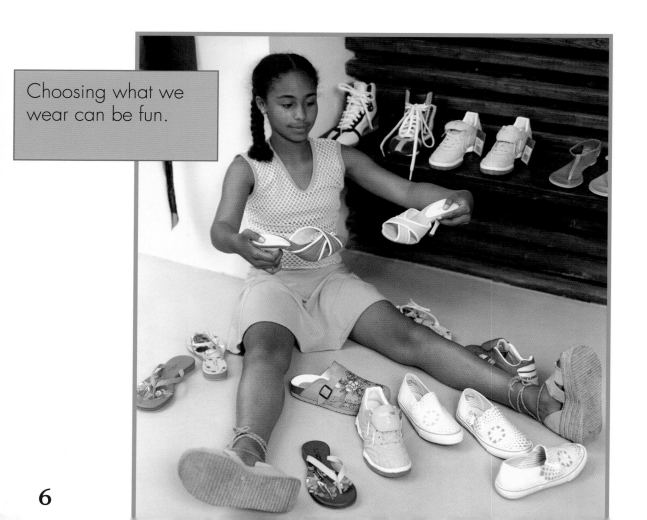

Choosing what we wear can be fun.

Other choices affect our happiness and safety. Our decisions can affect the happiness and safety of other people, too. These choices need a lot of careful thought.

Some choices are very important.

Choosing to Think for Yourself

Sometimes your friends might have **opinions** that are different from your own. For instance, they might like a different color or prefer a different game.

Friends can like different things.

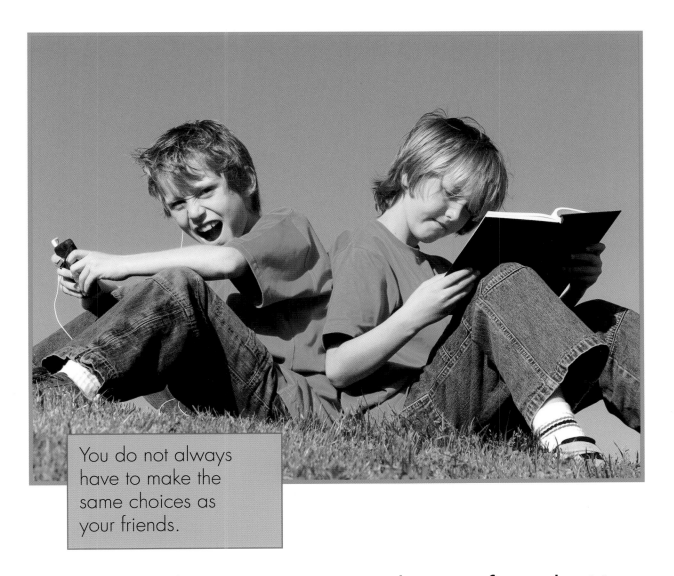

You do not always have to make the same choices as your friends.

You do not have to agree with your friends. You do not have to argue with them, either. It is fine to choose to disagree and just think differently. You do not always have to have the same opinions as your friends.

9

Choosing to Say "No"

Sometimes you may not feel happy about your friends' choices.

Sometimes your friends might choose to do something unkind or dangerous. You can choose to follow them, or you can choose to say "no" and do something different. This can be a hard choice to make.

If a friend tries to make you hurt someone else, it is better to walk away.

There may be times when people try to get you to do something that you know is wrong. You might be afraid that if you do not join in, they will be mean to you. If you feel like this, it is best to stop spending time with these people. It is important to have friends who make good choices and help you to make good choices, too.

Choosing to Be Friendly

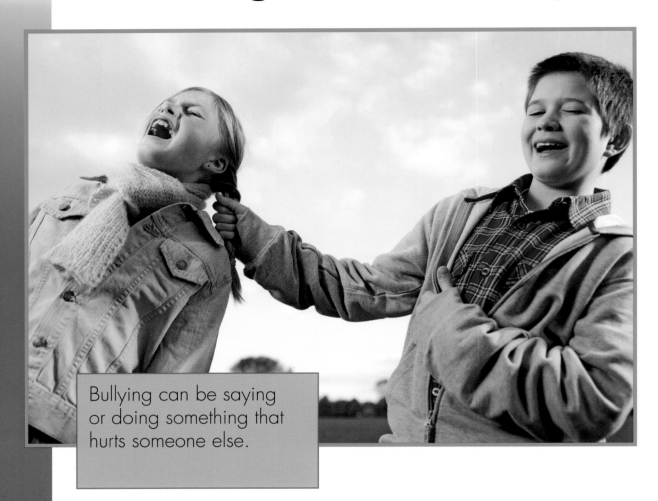

Bullying can be saying or doing something that hurts someone else.

Every day, we can choose how we behave toward other people. Being unfriendly to someone again and again can make them feel sad and hurt. This sort of behavior is called bullying.

When someone is bullying you, you might be afraid to tell anyone. Keeping bullying a secret would probably make you feel very unhappy. If you choose to tell an adult whom you **trust**, he or she will help to stop the bullying and help you feel much better.

Sharing your problems is a good choice.

Choosing to Be Fair

Every day, we have to choose whether or not to be **fair** toward others. For example, do you think it is fair for you to always demand to get your own way? Is it fair if you always choose which television programs to watch?

How does it feel when someone else makes all the choices?

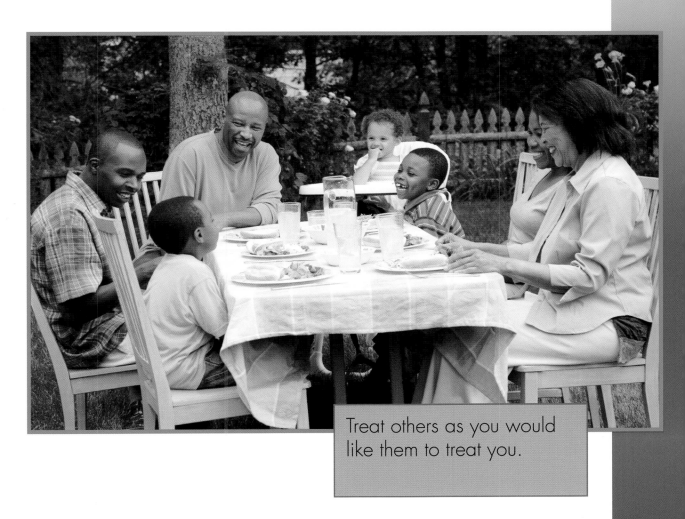

Treat others as you would like them to treat you.

If you make a choice that is not fair, you will make other people feel angry or unhappy. Would you like to feel like this? Often, we can make fair choices by thinking about what other people might want.

15

Choosing What to Eat

People have to make choices about what food to eat. Lots of foods are tasty, but some are better than others for giving your body **energy** and helping you stay well. Fruits, vegetables, and whole-grain foods are all healthy choices. Chips and candy are less healthy choices.

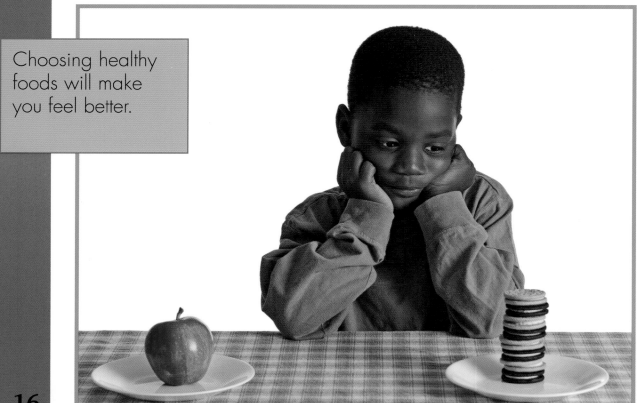

Choosing healthy foods will make you feel better.

Here are some foods that are not very healthy if you eat lots of them all the time. Next to each one is a healthier food that you could choose instead.

🚫 Unhealthy choices	✔ Healthy choice
Cookies	Cereal bars
Cake	Rice cakes
Candy	Dried fruit
French fries and ketchup	Vegetable sticks and dip
Chips	Nuts
Ice cream	Frozen yogurt
Soda	Fruit smoothie

Think about it

How do you feel if you eat too much candy or too many cookies? Do you feel better when you have eaten more healthy foods?

Choosing to Spend or Save Money

When you have pocket money to spend, it is important to make good choices about what you buy. It is better to buy things that last for a longer time, such as comics and toys, than to buy things that last for a short time, such as candy. Every time you spend money you need to think about these choices.

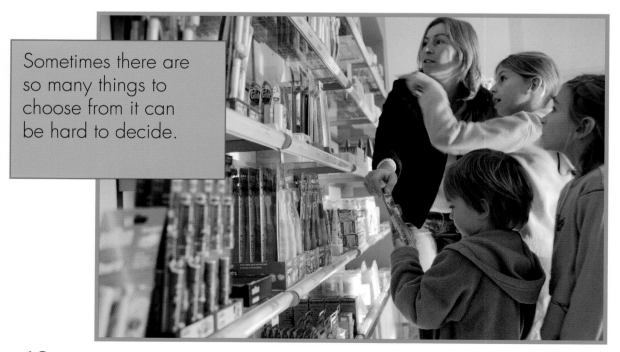

Sometimes there are so many things to choose from it can be hard to decide.

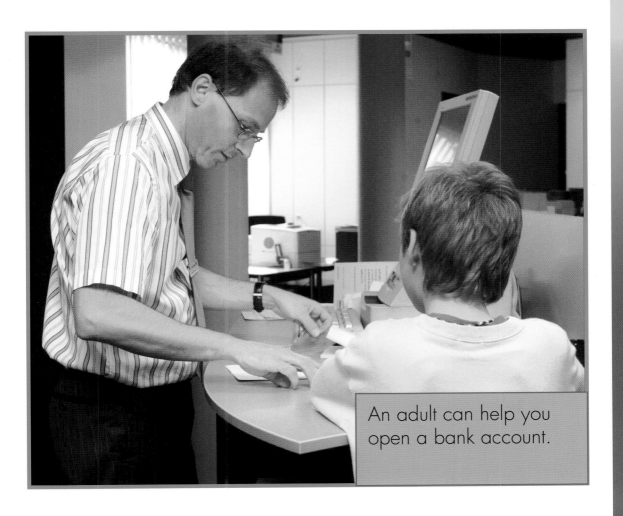

An adult can help you open a bank account.

You might choose to save your money instead. You could store up small amounts in a piggy bank or special box. For larger amounts, you could choose to keep your money safe in a bank account.

Choosing Entertainment

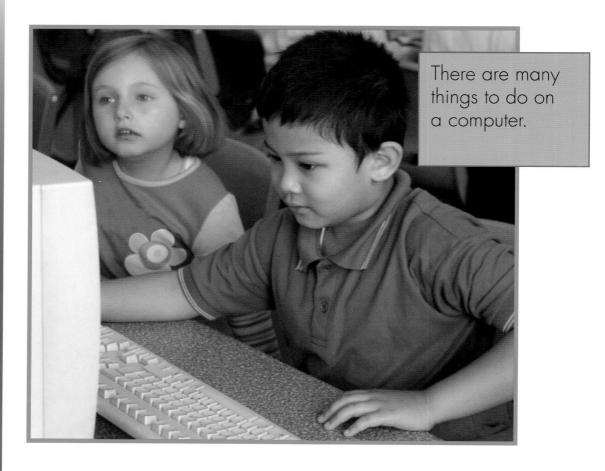

There are many things to do on a computer.

In your free time you might like reading books, watching television programs and DVDs, or playing computer games. When we choose types of entertainment that are right for our age, they can be a lot of fun.

If we choose entertainment that is meant for adults, we might find it confusing or even scary and upsetting. This is why adults sometimes ask us not to watch or play with certain things. If you are not sure whether something is right for you or not, ask a **trusted** adult to help you choose.

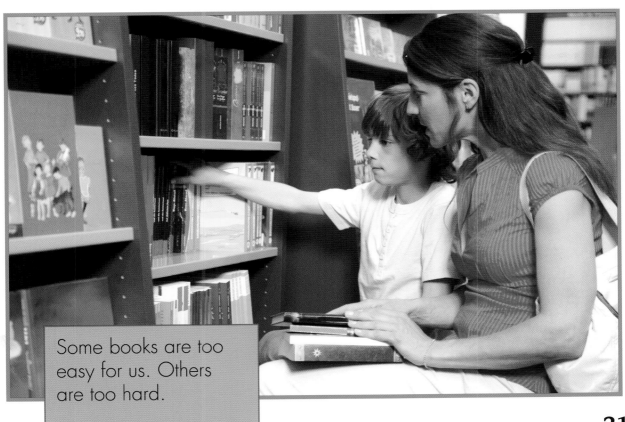

Some books are too easy for us. Others are too hard.

Choosing to Be Active

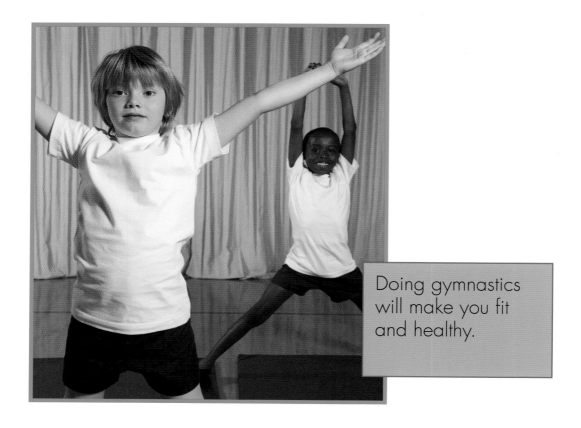

Doing gymnastics will make you fit and healthy.

Activities like running, skipping, jumping, dancing, dog-walking, and soccer make you feel full of **energy** and keep you healthy. Choosing to do one of these activities is a great way to spend your spare time. Think about which activity you would pick as your favorite.

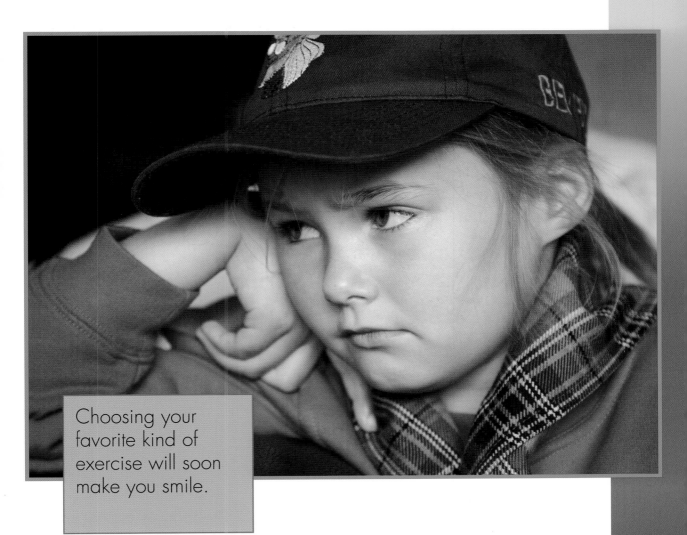

Choosing your favorite kind of exercise will soon make you smile.

If you choose not to get any exercise, you will feel lazy and become unfit. You may become bored and grumpy, too. Doing your favorite activity will soon make you feel much better.

Choosing to Follow the Rules

Sometimes people give us **rules** to follow. These rules are usually set for a good reason, such as to keep us safe. For example, at home, you might have rules about things you are not allowed to touch. It is important to choose to follow these rules so you do not get hurt.

Adults set rules because they care about you.

At school, there are also many rules to follow. They are there to make life **fair**, safe, and happy for everyone, so it is a good idea to choose to follow them. Here are some typical school rules. Think about what might happen if you ignored them.

- ✓ no cheating on tests
- ✓ no running in the hallways
- ✓ no cell phones during class
- ✓ no swinging backward on the chairs
- ✓ no copying other people's work

Choosing to Tell the Truth

Sometimes things go wrong and it is our fault.
It might happen by accident or on purpose.
It is important to choose to tell the truth, even
when it may seem easier to tell a lie or to blame
someone else.

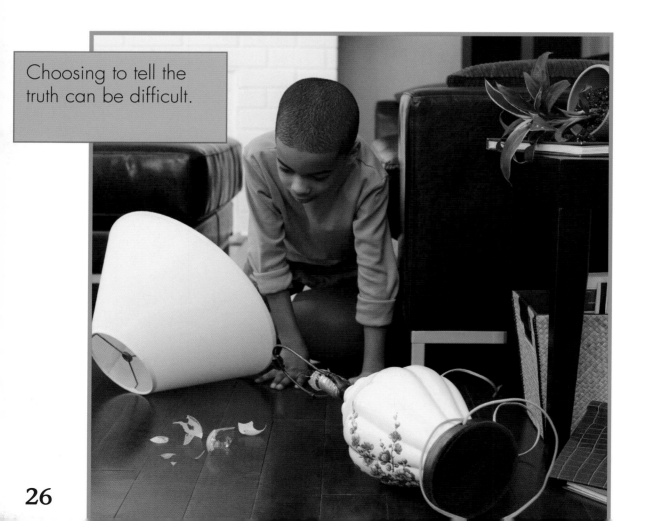

Choosing to tell the truth can be difficult.

Choosing to hide the truth can make you feel miserable.

If you do not tell the truth, you might feel guilty and worried. And if people find out the truth, they may be angry with you. It is always a better choice to tell the truth. Even if adults are upset about what you have done, they will be pleased with you for being **honest** and for taking **responsibility**.

Making Choices and Happiness

It is important to make good choices so that you and others can stay happy and safe, and so that other people **trust** you.

Good choices include:

- ☑ thinking about other people, not just ourselves
- ☑ choosing to share and take turns
- ☑ choosing to help out at home
- ☑ choosing to try our best with everything
- ☑ choosing to be **honest**
- ☑ choosing to think for ourselves and not do things we know are wrong

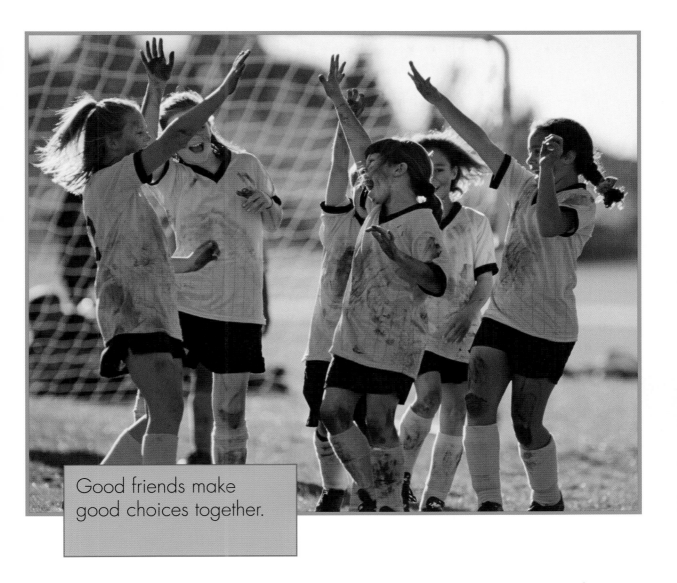

Good friends make good choices together.

Making good choices will mean that your life is easier and more enjoyable. You will help yourself and other people to be happy and stay safe.

Glossary

energy power to play and work and do everything you want and need to do

fair if you behave fairly, you treat everybody the same

honest truthful, able to be trusted

opinion point of view; thoughts about something or someone

responsibility thing that it is your job to do

right basic rule of good behavior that people should show toward you, such as being fair, thoughtful, and safe. Everyone else has these rights, too.

rule instruction that tells you what you are or are not allowed to do

trust belief that someone will do the right thing

Find Out More

Books

Loewen, Nancy. *Do I Have To?: Kids Talk About Responsibility.* Mankato, Minn.: Picture Window, 2003.

Mayer, Cassie. *Being Honest.* Chicago: Heinemann Library, 2008.

Mayer, Cassie. *Following Rules.* Chicago: Heinemann Library, 2008.

Nettleton, Pamela Hill. *Is That True?: Kids Talk About Honesty.* Mankato, Minn.: Picture Window, 2005.

Small, Mary. *Being a Good Citizen: A Book About Citizenship.* Mankato, Minn.: Picture Window, 2006.

Website

www.hud.gov/kids

This government Website shows children what it means to be good citizens.

Index